For Freddie

First published in 2009 in Great Britain by
Barrington Stoke Ltd
18 Walker Street, Edinburgh, EH3 7LP

www.barringtonstoke.co.uk

This edition published 2012

ISBN: 978-1-78112-090-3

Printed in China by Leo

The Fix

by

Sophie McKenzie

Contents

Chapter 1

First to Score

Blake stood in front of the tall steel gates. There were bars across them, and a big chain and padlock. A KEEP OUT sign hung on the front.

"OK, man," Blake said softly. He grinned and looked at his friend, Dan. "Let's break in."

Dan grabbed the middle bar of the gate. He pulled himself up onto the top and jumped down. A second later Blake was clambering up after him. In two swift moves he was at the top of the gate. He saw Dan waiting below him.

"Quick," Dan whispered. "There might be a security guard."

Blake nodded. But he didn't climb down – he stared ahead. In front of the gate was a line of turn-stiles. Beyond those lay the curved roof of the stadium. And beyond that was the pitch.

It was dark but Blake knew the grass would be in perfect condition. Just as he knew that the stadium building gleamed with fresh paint and the seats in the stands were unscuffed and unbroken.

This was the Holton City Stadium. It had been built in Holton City, with some Lottery money and money from local business. It was brand new – a home for all the local football teams, from Second Division Holton City, to the City Colts team Blake played for.

"Blake, will you friggin' hurry up?" Dan whispered.

Blake shook himself and climbed down the gate.

"Where now?" Dan said.

Blake thought for a second. Their plan had been to explore the stadium. No one had played any matches here yet. In fact it wasn't open to the public for another ten days. The opening match was going to be the final of the Colts Cup – a tournament for all the Colts teams in the region.

"The pitch, man," Blake said. "I wanna be the first person to score a goal on the new pitch."

"Yeah, man." Dan laughed. "Except *I'm* gonna be the first one to score."

"Oh, yeah?"

They raced to the turn-stiles, then scrambled over them. A dog barked in the distance.

Dan grabbed Blake's arm. "What was that?"

"Just a dog." Blake grinned. "Miles away."

"Well, let's keep the noise down," Dan whispered. "OK?"

They charged up some stairs, along the top of the stand, then down onto the pitch. The grass shone in the moonlight. Blake yanked his bag off his back and pulled out his football. His heart thumped hard and fast as he dropped the ball onto the pitch and kicked it towards the Holton end.

Dan dived forward in a clumsy tackle. Blake tapped the ball sideways, then did a swift step-over. He kicked the ball again, harder this time. It flew up the pitch. Blake raced after it, speeding up as he ran. Every part of him was focused on the ball. This was what he loved. This was when he came alive. When it was just him and the ball.

"Oi! Blake! Wait." Dan's heavy foot-steps pounded up the pitch.

Blake was sure he could out-run Dan to the goal. Dan was a good defender. But Blake was the fastest runner on their team. Holton City Colts' star striker. If City Colts won the Semi-Final on Saturday, he would be playing here, on this pitch, in the Final in ten days' time.

The sound of a siren blasted across the pitch. Blake spun round. "What the hell's that?"

Dan was fumbling in his pocket. He pulled out his phone. The siren noise sounded again. Even louder.

"Is that your *ring tone?*" Blake asked.

Dan pressed at his mobile, frantic to shut it up. The siren noise stopped.

"Nice one, Dan." Blake made a face. "I thought you said to keep the noise down?"

"D'you think anyone heard?" Dan looked round, his eyes big and scared.

Blake gave a sigh. "I don't think anyone's here, so no." He looked more closely at the phone. "Is that new?"

"Yeah, it's a video phone. The best on the market for ..." Dan stopped.

Dan's face went red and he turned away. He was always getting new stuff. He had his own laptop at home and always wore the latest football gear.

Blake was lucky if he got a new pair of boots when his feet grew. It wasn't his mum's fault. Just that his dad never sent her any money.

Dan kicked the ball up the pitch, then ran after it.

"Oi, pass it, man," Blake yelled. He was annoyed he'd let Dan win the ball. "Pass it."

Dan got to the edge of the penalty area. He smashed the ball. It sailed past Blake, into the corner of the net.

"Yeees!" Dan's cry rang out round the stadium.

"Ssssh!" Blake sighed. He didn't feel much like congratulating Dan but he had to admit it had been a great goal. "Nice shot," he said. "Power *and* accuracy. Might even impress Coach."

Dan grinned. "Nearly as good as that goal you scored against the Tigers last month."

Blake shrugged. He always got embarrassed when people talked about the goals he'd scored. But Dan was right. That volley he'd made on the turn in the match against the Tigers had been pretty cool. His good mood soared back. He ran up the pitch, so as to fetch the ball out of the goal. But at that minute, a dog barked. It sounded close.

He turned. Dan was a few yards away, his mouth open with horror.

And then, behind Dan, Blake saw it – a large guard dog. It was inside the stadium, leaping onto the pitch, running straight towards them.

"Get them, Bullitt," shouted a deep, male voice. "Go on, boy. Get the bloody vandals."

Blake's heart pounded. "Leg it," he yelled. "Run!"

Chapter 2
Mr Vilman

Blake got to the edge of the pitch. He jumped across the barrier and onto the stand, then ran at top speed past the seats. His heart hammered in his chest. The dog was right behind him. Blake could hear the thump of his paws. He ran harder. Up between the rows of seats to where the stand roof hung low. He jumped up and gripped the edge of the roof. He pulled himself up and crawled over to where the roof flattened out.

Now he could no longer see the dog. But he could still hear it and it was going berserk just under the roof where Blake crouched. He could see a large man in track pants crossing the pitch towards the stand. No sign of Dan. The man had a limp and he was swearing – and panting as he ran.

"Good boy, Bullitt," he shouted. "Keep 'em there."

Blake flattened himself against the roof. He heard the man's foot-steps. Then his voice. He sounded puzzled.

"Where are they, then, boy? Which way did they go?"

Blake held his breath.

After what seemed like an hour but couldn't have been more than a minute, the barking stopped. The man led the dog back across the pitch, grumbling as he limped away.

Blake didn't want to risk going back the way he had come. He crawled along the roof until he got to the other side – away from the pitch. There was still no sign of Dan. Had he got out all right?

All Blake needed to do now was get down and stick close to the wall around the stadium until he found another gate to climb over.

The roof on this side was further from the ground. Blake took a deep breath and jumped. He landed with a light thud.

Yes. There was a gate – just a few metres away.

"It was one of the guard dogs," said a man's voice from somewhere close by. "Stop changing the subject."

"OK." Another man's voice. "But I *have* paid you."

Blake froze. The voices were coming from a small open window. Blake twisted his head a little to see through the window. He could just make out the side of a man's head. Dark, slicked-back hair. The collar of a sharply cut suit.

"What about the *rest* of the money, Mr Vilman?" the first, angry voice said.

Blake shivered. He knew he should just turn and go, but something held him there. He shuffled up closer to the window so he could see more of the room inside.

It was one of the changing rooms. The dark-haired man – he must be Mr Vilman – was walking up and down with his hands in his suit trousers.

"I'll nick the money from the stadium savings account," he said. "Like I did before. I just need more time."

"Right." The other speaker snorted. He was also in a suit. Shorter than Mr Vilman. The electric strip light above the row of lockers by the far wall glinted off his balding head. "I'll give you two weeks, Mr Vilman," he said. "That's all the extension you're getting. Then I want my money."

The man turned and marched out. Mr Vilman shook his head and swore under his breath.

Blake edged away. He kept close to the shadow of the changing room wall as he padded towards the gate. Who was this Mr Vilman? And what was he talking about?

Nicking money from the stadium savings account – that ... that was stealing.

Blake looked round. He was just past the changing room door. The gate was opposite. There was no sound from inside.

He darted towards the gate. His ring tone smashed into the silence. *No*. He'd totally forgotten his phone was on.

He fumbled in his jeans pocket and pulled it out. It was Dan. Blake stabbed at the phone. The noise stopped. And then a load of things happened at once.

The door of the changing rooms flung open with a bang. A strip of light flooded his path to the gate.

"Who's there?" someone shouted.

Blake turned round. It was Mr Vilman. His face was thin and pinched, with hard, cold blue eyes.

"Who the hell are ...?" Mr Vilman began.

Blake turned and ran. He was at the gate in seconds. He hurled himself up and over the top.

Mr Vilman's voice rang out. "I'll find you, you little scum. I'll get you."

Heart pounding, Blake dropped to the ground on the other side of the gate. He raced away. He didn't stop running until he was three streets away from the stadium. Then he slowed to a jog for the last minute home.

He let himself in, plodded upstairs and threw himself on the bed. Mr Vilman had stolen money from the stadium savings account and was planning on taking more. And Blake had overheard him talking about it.

He could still hear Mr Vilman shouting at him *"I'll find you. I'll get you,"* he'd said.

Blake's heart began to slow down. That was all rubbish. How could Mr Vilman find him? He didn't even know who Blake was.

A feeling of huge relief flooded through him. He'd done it. He'd got away.

He rang Dan. They had a laugh about the security man and his dog. Dan had got out fast, no problem, then he'd rung Blake. That was the call that had messed everything up. Blake didn't tell him why he hadn't picked up.

Or what he'd overheard at the changing rooms. He needed time to think about it.

"Man, that was cool," Dan said.

Blake laughed.

"Gotta go," Dan said. "My mum's yelling at me for something. Hey, man, sorry you lost your ball. See ya tomorrow."

The phone went dead. Blake didn't move. The ball. He'd forgotten about his football. It must still be on the pitch, in the back of the goal, where Dan had kicked it.

Everything else faded away. It was as if a cold hand reached inside him and was squeezing the air out of his lungs. Mr Vilman would find that ball. Which meant he'd see what Blake could see in his head right now. The bit of the ball where Blake had written his name. *Blake Johnson*, it said, in clear black letters.

Chapter 3
The Offer

The next day was Thursday. The last Thursday of the month.

"No money from your dad *again*, Blake," Mum said from his bedroom doorway. She sounded like she'd been crying.

Blake pulled the duvet over his head. He hated it when Mum got upset like that. Why did she go on expecting Dad to send them anything? Dad was long gone and all taken up with a new family. For Blake, Dad was out of the picture for good. He and Mum had to look after themselves.

The bed creaked as Mum sat down, making a dip in the mattress. Blake's legs slid towards the dip. He peered over the top of the duvet.

Mum's bottom lip was wobbling.

Blake stared at her, feeling helpless.

She looked round. "Oh, Blake ... I don't want to get you all upset with your big match coming up on Saturday but I'm just so worried ..." Mum sniffed back her tears.

Blake had forgotten. There'd been too much else to think about. The Colts Cup Semi-Final was in just two days' time. And he was playing. Blake felt a thrill of excitement, then a pang of guilt as he looked at Mum's face.

"We'll be all right, Mum," he said as he sat up in bed and gave her a hug.

"That's just it, Blake," Mum said. "I don't think we will this time. If I don't get £300 fast I'll be under on the rent *again*. If that happens we're going to have to move to Nanny Mam's."

"What?" Blake sat back, shocked. Nanny Mam lived miles away. She was old and her house smelled. Plus, there was no decent football team anywhere near her ... not even a kid's team. "No way, Mum!" he said. "Why can't you borrow the money ... get a loan or something?"

Mum turned on him. "I won't go into debt again, Blake. I've only just paid off all the money your dad left us owing."

"But ..."

"I don't want to hear it," Mum said firmly.

****

Blake spent all day worrying. Either he worried about having to move to Nanny Mam's or that Mr Vilman was going to track him down because of the name on his football. Twice the teachers shouted at him. He only just missed getting a detention for chewing some gum which he'd totally forgotten to take out after break. At last school was over and he and Dan headed for football practice.

As always, once Blake was on the pitch, all his worries dropped away. He was free, somehow, when he played football. The ball moved where and how he wanted it to. The other players were too slow to stop him. And space seemed to open up wherever he ran.

He scored twice. The second goal was a real beauty – a curving free kick from just outside the box.

"Nice one, Blake," Coach grunted.

Blake grinned. From Coach, that was top praise.

As he came off the pitch he felt better than he had done all day. And then he felt a hand on his shoulder.

"Blake Johnson?"

He looked round. There, standing behind him, was Mr Vilman. He held out Blake's football. "The security man found this. I think you left it behind on your little adventure last night."

Blake looked round. The rest of the squad were jogging ahead, eager to get home. Mr Vilman pushed the ball into Blake's hands. His blue eyes were cold and mean.

"Trespassing's a crime, you know," he hissed.

"We didn't do any damage," Blake said. He felt scared, but he stared back at Mr Vilman.

Mr Vilman looked older than he had done last night. There were lines round his eyes and streaks of grey in his slicked-back hair.

Mr Vilman came closer. "I know you heard me talking," he said.

"What, about stealing from the stadium savings account?" Blake bounced his football on the ground. "Yeah, I heard."

"I need ..." Mr Vilman clenched his fist. "I need to know you're not going to say anything to anyone."

Blake's chest tightened. That sounded like a threat.

"And what if I do tell someone?" he said, trying to stop his voice from shaking. "Like Holton City's bosses ...?"

"I haven't come here to hurt you, Blake." Mr Vilman smiled – a thin, nasty smile. "I've come here to offer you money. Lots of money."

"Money?" Blake bounced the football again. "What, to stop me telling people you're a thief?"

Mr Vilman grabbed the ball. "Not exactly," he said. And then he smiled. "I want to pay you to fix the match on Saturday, so that Holton City Colts loses the Semi-Final."

Chapter 4
The Fix

Blake stared at Mr Vilman. Did he mean what he was saying? Blake shook his head and edged away.

"Problem, Blake?" Coach strode over. He looked hard at Mr Vilman. "Who's this?"

Mr Vilman held out his hand. "Martin Vilman – friend of Blake's family. I run a local import business."

Blake opened his mouth to tell Coach that wasn't true. Then he shut it again. What did

Mr Vilman mean about 'fixing' the match? What did he mean by 'lots' of money?

Coach turned to look at Blake.

"Everything's cool, Coach," Blake said.

"Fine." Coach turned and jogged off the pitch. "Don't be late on Saturday," he shouted as he got into his car.

Blake watched Coach drive off. He could see a few of his team mates chatting to each other as they waited for their lifts home.

"Let me explain," Mr Vilman said. "I'll give you £300 right here, right now, if you agree to cock up all the chances you get to score on Saturday. Then another £300 afterwards. Deal?"

Blake frowned. "How's that going to work?" he said. "I'm a striker. If I don't play properly I'll just be taken off the pitch."

Mr Vilman laughed. "I've been finding out about you, Blake. You're Holton City Colts' *star striker*. I think you'll be let off a few poor shots before anyone thinks it's a good idea to sub you."

"But ..." Blake shook his head. "I don't get it. How does this help you?"

"I don't think that's any of your business," Vilman muttered.

"Well, I do." Blake crossed his arms. Mr Vilman was looking across at the football pitch. The sun was low behind the far goal now – another fifteen minutes and it would be dark.

There was a long pause.

"I have debts, OK, Blake?" Mr Vilman said. "If I make a private bet on Holton City Colts to lose the Semi-Final and you make sure that happens, then I'll win my bet. At the moment Holton are favourites so the odds are in my favour. If I bet enough money, I'll win enough to pay off my debts. See? It's simple."

Blake stared at him. Mr Vilman made what he was planning sound so simple, like it was the most normal thing in the world. "But ... but fixing the match like that ... it's cheating," he said at last.

Mr Vilman laughed. "I prefer to see it as taking control. At least it means I don't need to take any more money from the stadium account."

Blake stood still, his mind spinning. £300 was the exact amount of money Mum needed for the rent. This was his chance to help her, to make sure they could stay on in Holton. It was like fate. Like it was meant to be. Except ...

"It's wrong," Blake said flatly. He turned away.

"No." Mr Vilman grabbed his arm. "It's right. This way, everyone wins. I get my money. You get your money. And Holton City Colts get to say they didn't lose until the Semi-Final and that there's always next year's tournament."

Blake stared at Mr Vilman.

"£300 now. £300 after the match," Mr Vilman said.

Another £300 would mean Mum didn't have to worry about next month's rent either.

"No. It's wrong. It's cheating," Blake said.

"OK." Mr Vilman let go of his arm. "Why don't we play for it? Penalty shoot-out. Me in goal. If you score, you walk away and tell anyone you like what you heard me say about stealing the stadium funds. I'll deny it, of course, and by the time anyone proves anything I'll be long gone. No one wins. But if you miss or I save the goal, you agree to fix the match on Saturday. You earn yourself £600. Everyone wins. Deal?"

Blake shuffled from foot to foot. What should he do? "Do you even play football?" he asked at last.

"Used to." Mr Vilman's eyes glinted. "Not a bad mid-fielder, back then. Nothing next to you, of course."

Blake frowned. He was sure he could score past the man. Mr Vilman was well old. Over 40 at least. Blake hadn't missed a penalty in two seasons.

"So if I get the ball in the net, you'll let me walk away and say what I like?" Blake said.

Mr Vilman nodded. He backed away, Blake's football in his hands. "But if you miss,"

he said, "you earn yourself £300 on the spot."
He turned and jogged into the goal mouth.

Blake strolled up to the penalty spot.
Maybe this was the best way. Leave the
decision up to chance.

Mr Vilman took off his smart black jacket
and folded it neatly. He laid it by the side of
the goal, then kicked the ball towards Blake.

Blake steadied the ball with his toe. He
stepped back. Mr Vilman slicked back his hair.

Blake stared at the ball. Which way should
he send it? He knew exactly how to disguise
what he was doing.

"£300, Blake. Right now," Mr Vilman called.
"Take your time."

Blake took a deep breath. This was it. He
could whack the ball in the top corner, just like
he'd done so many times before. Then he'd
walk away. Everything would be like it was
before he and Dan broke into the stadium.

Or he could miss. Send the ball wide of the
goal.

He steadied himself for the short run he was going to take.

Miss. Score. Miss. Score.

He ran forward, eyes on the goal.

Miss. Score. Miss. Score.

His foot made contact with the ball. Badly. A toe poke. Accurate, but no power. The ball rolled towards the centre of the goal. Mr Vilman scooped it up, easily.

"Well done, son," he said. "That was the right decision."

"I didn't mean ..." But Blake couldn't finish the sentence. Because it wasn't true. He *had* meant to miss.

He wanted Mr Vilman's money.

Chapter 5
The Semi-Final

It was Saturday. The Semi-Final. Blake's stomach churned as he walked out onto the pitch for the warm-up. He saw Mum right away. She was in the seats to the left of the Holton City Colts goal, wearing a red scarf. She waved at him and grinned.

Blake's heart sank. Everything had felt wrong since he'd taken Mr Vilman's money. He couldn't put his finger on what the matter was, just that nothing felt right any more. Take Mum. When he'd handed over the £300 she looked like she might faint, she was so shocked.

"But where did you get it, sweet-heart? Where did it come from?" she kept asking.

Blake had told her the story he'd planned. That he'd won the money on some fantasy football game. And Mum had bought the lie. Totally bought it.

"Oi, Blake, wake up!" Dan shouted from the box.

Blake jumped. "What?" he yelled.

"Pass the ball, you idiot."

"Yeah, come on, man," someone else shouted.

Blake looked down. The ball was at his feet. Dan and the other two defenders were staring at him.

"Sorry," he called. He kicked the ball over to them and ran towards the middle of the pitch. Another ball was in play there. The team captain and a group of mid-fielders were warming up.

Blake joined in but he didn't feel right. The ground they were playing in was much smaller than the new stadium. Just a few banks of seats on both sides of the pitch. Most of the people who'd come to watch were standing. A good crowd, but no more than 100 people, tops. Blake thought of the new stadium. That could seat ten thousand.

With a pang Blake remembered that if he lost this, the Semi-Final, he wouldn't get to play the Final in the big stadium after all.

Blake looked round again. No sign of Mr Vilman.

The ref's whistle blew and the teams took their places, ready to begin.

Blake's marker was the centre back for the opposing team. No taller than Blake, but bigger and heavier. He moved with surprising speed. Blake got to the ball. The centre back tackled him and Blake came alive. His feet skipped over the defender's leg, his spikes just grazing the guy's shin.

He got the ball. Kicked it on. *Wham*. A foot hooked round his ankle. His leg was

yanked back. The ground flew up to meet him.
He lay on the grass, gasping for breath. The
defender who had tripped him stood over him,
holding out his hand.

"All right, mate?" he grinned.

Arsehole. Blake jumped to his feet, blood
pumping through his head. He pushed at the
defender's chest, just as the ref's whistle blew.
The defender lunged for Blake. Blake skipped
back.

The referee pounded up, panting. He called
both boys over. For a second Blake thought he
was going to be carded, but the ref just wanted
to give out a warning.

"Watch it." The ref turned from Blake to
the defender. "I've got my eye on both of you.
Let's have a clean game."

Blake nodded. He shook the defender's
hand as quickly as possible.

As he jogged away, panic filled his chest.
He'd nearly got himself sent off and the game
had hardly started. What would Mr Vilman
make of that?

He'd probably demand the £300 back, at the very least.

With a jolt, Blake knew he had to play badly. That he couldn't let Mum down.

For the rest of that half it was easy to mess up his chances. The other side were good. The centre back he'd nearly got into a fight with marked him well. Blake hardly got a touch on the ball. When he was sent a couple of decent passes, he miss-hit them.

At the very end of the first half, both teams scored. When the half-time whistle blew, Blake walked slowly off the pitch. Had anyone noticed that he was off-form?

It didn't take long to find out.

"A load of blinking balls," Coach yelled at them in the changing room. "No one's creating chances. Defence seems to have decided they're at some kind of ladies' tea-party. And as for you ..." Coach rounded on Blake. "You had two great chances and you cocked up both of them."

Blake looked down at his boots. "Sorry, Coach."

"Sorry's not good enough!" Coach shouted. "Now, get out there and work for it."

Blake tried to look like he was working hard through the second half. He ran around a lot and won the ball a few times, then let his game go soft. The score stayed at one-all for most of the second half. Then, towards the end, Blake won his team a corner.

The captain took it. A perfect curving kick into the box, where the ball landed at Blake's feet. He looked up. The goal was just a metre away. The opposition goalie ran towards him. In that second Blake forgot to think. His feet seemed to move for him. In an instant, he'd side-stepped the goalie and tapped the ball home.

Yeees!

His team mates were all over him, hugging him and patting him on the back. Yells of joy filled his ears. Blake grinned. He'd scored the winning goal. He punched his fist in the air and ran back up the field.

A line of Holton City Colts supporters were jumping up and down.

"We're through to the Final," one shouted. "We're gonna win the cup."

That was when Blake saw Mr Vilman, standing at the end of the row. His eyes were narrowed, staring right at Blake. His arms were folded.

He wasn't smiling.

Chapter 6
The Hero

Blake was a hero.

He lost track of how many people came up to him after that Saturday Semi-Final and patted him on the back, or grinned and told him what a fantastic goal he'd scored.

But all Blake could see was Mr Vilman's angry face. All he could hear was Mr Vilman's voice in his ear from the very first time they'd met. *"I'll find you. I'll get you."*

He'd expected Mr Vilman to come up to him after the match, but there was no sign of him.

Blake stayed in on Saturday evening and all day Sunday. He looked out for Mr Vilman on the way to school on Monday morning and all the way to football practice that evening. But nothing happened.

It was only on the way home from football that Blake started to think maybe he'd got away with it. Maybe Mr Vilman wasn't going to come after him after all.

"Hey, Blake, did you see Coach's face when I did that sliding tackle on Fred Smith?" Dan raced along the pavement, then twisted round, leg out to one side, to show what he'd done.

"Yeah, man." Blake grinned. He wasn't sure Coach had been as impressed by the tackle as Dan thought, but he didn't want to trash Dan's good mood.

"Hey, tomorrow after practice we're meeting up at the park." Dan stopped at the corner of his road. "Those girls from Fred's party are gonna be there. You interested?"

"Sure." Blake watched Dan race off, then took the next left turn into his own street. He walked along happily, lost in his thoughts.

What was Mum cooking for tea? Would the set piece that Coach showed them today really work? Was that girl from Fred's party, with the long legs and the sparkly eyes, going to be at the park tomorrow?

He got to his front door and turned the key.

"Hi, Mum."

"Hi, Blake," Mum called. "We're in the living room."

Blake gave a sigh. Who was 'we'? Probably one of Mum's friends. Well, he hoped they weren't staying long. He was starving.

"Come and see who it is, Blake," Mum said. She sounded excited.

With another sigh, Blake dumped his football bag and opened the living room door.

His mouth dropped open. There on the sofa, a cup of tea in his hand, sat Mr Vilman.

Mr Vilman smiled. Mum stood up. She beamed at Blake.

"This is Mr Vilman. He's one of the Holton City Football Club bosses. He's been telling me how much he rates your goal-scoring," Mum said. "Thinks you have real talent."

Blake stared at Mr Vilman. What was going on?

"Hi, Blake." Mr Vilman looked at Blake and smiled again. "I just popped by to tell your mother that now that I've *found* you I'm going to keep my eye on you."

"Right." Blake's heart beat faster.

Mum's eyes sparkled. "Mr Vilman, that's very kind of you," she said.

"I like to do what I can to help local talent." Mr Vilman said as he sat back. "You never know," he went on, looking hard at Blake, "where people will end up."

"Would you like some more tea?" Mum was already at the door.

"Yes, thank you," Mr Vilman said. He kept his cold, blue eyes on Blake.

Blake stood, fixed to the spot as Mum went out to make the tea.

"I ... er ..." Blake began.

"Save it, Blake." The smile fell from Mr Vilman's face. He got up and shut the door. "What the hell were you playing at, scoring that goal? I thought we had a deal."

"I didn't … I … I, er …" Blake's heart was pounding now. "I'll pay the money back. I …"

"Don't play games with me," Mr Vilman snapped. "Your mum's already told me how you helped her out with the rent this month. It's a shame …" He stopped for a minute. "She seems like a nice lady."

"What d'you mean?" Blake couldn't believe what was happening. He'd thought Mr Vilman would find him on a dark street or down some empty alley. But not this, not here, in his home, with his mum.

"I mean," Mr Vilman said with a nasty look in his eyes, "that as you can't pay the money back, you have two choices. Listen carefully. One – you play badly in the Cup Final next week. If you make sure your team lose, I'll win back the money I lost in the Semi-Final and I'll still be able to pay off my – "

"No way!" The words burst out of Blake. "I can't – "

"Wait ..." Mr Vilman curled his lip. "You haven't heard the second choice. Like I said, your mum seems like a nice lady ..."

Blake froze. "What?"

Mr Vilman gave a sigh. "I mean, it would be a shame if she got hurt."

Blake stared at him. Did Vilman mean he'd hurt Mum if Blake played well and his team won?

"You need to understand how important this is, Blake." Mr Vilman's voice dropped to a whisper. "I know you're the man of the house. It's up to you to keep your mum from getting hurt ... in any way. Isn't it?"

Mr Vilman walked out. Blake could hear him telling Mum he didn't have time for the second cup of tea any more, and Mum chattering back politely. Blake put his hands over his face.

Mum was in danger. And it was all his fault.

What the hell was he going to do now?

Chapter 7
Like Father, Like Son

Blake played so badly at football practice the next day that Coach said he might have to drop him from the Final on Saturday.

At first Blake felt pleased. After all, if he didn't play, he couldn't try and lose the match. But when he thought about it, he knew that not playing wouldn't go down any better with Mr Vilman than if he played to win. And that it'd still mean Mum getting hurt. Only this time there'd be no money.

After practice, Blake walked to the park with his friends. The only way that Mum would be safe was if Blake lost the match for his team – on purpose. At least that way he'd earn the last £300. Maybe Mum wouldn't need all of it. Maybe he could spend some of it on stuff for his team mates – they didn't need to know why he was spending money on them, but it would be a way of him making up for what he'd done.

They reached the park. "Hey, Blake, look." Dan's shout stopped Blake thinking about the mess he was in. He looked over to where Dan was pointing.

On the other side of the kids' playground was the Youth Club. Beyond that was a broken-down old shed.

No one Blake knew ever went inside the Youth Club. But he and his friends often met up at the shed and the patch of woodland beside it. Right now a huge group of people their age, including loads of girls, were standing outside the shed.

"Looking good, man." Dan laughed.

Blake walked over with the others. The girl he'd liked from Fred's party wasn't there. Just his luck. He tried talking to a few other people, but he couldn't relax.

In the end, he drifted away, into the trees. The wind had dropped and the voices chattering away by the shed carried in the night air. Blake leaned against a tree and listened to bits of what people were saying. Guys talking about some football match. Girls giggling over what someone was wearing.

These people had *nothing* to worry about. Blake had never felt so alone. He turned and walked deeper into the wood. The voices faded to a murmur.

There was a rustling in the bushes behind him. Blake turned swiftly, his whole body tensed. There was someone in the shadows. Was it Mr Vilman?

The person moved closer. Blake saw who it was. Dan.

"You prat, Dan," he said. "You shouldn't creep up on people like that."

"What's the matter?" Dan said.

"What d'you mean?"

"You. You're, like, all boring and miserable," Dan went on. "What's up?"

Blake shrugged. "Nothing."

"Come on, Blake." Dan rolled his eyes. "You've been acting weird ever since the Semi-Final." He stopped. "No ... no, it's been going on longer than that. You've been weird ever since ... since we broke into the new stadium."

Blake turned away, so Dan couldn't see his face.

"Did something happen then?" Dan asked.

Blake stood, staring down at the ground. The air was still all around them. Dan's words hung in the silence.

"Right," Dan said. "Don't talk to me."

Blake could hear Dan turning, walking away.

"Wait," Blake shouted. "Listen."

It only took a few minutes to tell Dan everything.

"So, you see," Blake finished, "I don't have a choice. I've got to play badly in the Final."

There was a long silence, then Dan looked up. "No, I don't see that at all."

"What?"

"I can't believe you took money to play badly," Dan said.

Anger welled up inside Blake. "That's all very well for you to say," he snapped. "I don't see you having to help your mum pay the rent." He pointed at Dan's video phone, sticking out of his shirt pocket. "All you have to worry about is which freakin' ring tone to download."

"That's not fair," Dan snapped back. "All I'm saying is that taking the bribe is where you went wrong. But you did the right thing afterwards – you scored that goal in the Semi. You just need to do that again in the Final and – "

"Have you listened to anything I've been saying?" Blake's voice shook with anger. "If I do that my mum will get hurt. And my dad's not around to look after her."

"That's rubbish. This Vilman, whoever he is – is just saying stuff to get you to do what he wants."

"No way," Blake said. "You haven't seen him. I wish I'd never told you – I might have known you wouldn't get it."

"Oh, yeah?" Dan took a step backwards. "My fault now, is it? That's so typical of you, man. Blame everyone else. Blame me. Blame your dad. Blame being poor. Blame Mr Bigshot Vilman. You're the one who took the bribe. You didn't have to do that. No one said anything about your mum getting hurt then."

"Piss off," Blake shouted. "You've got no idea, Dan. I was trying to help Mum. And it is my dad's fault. If he sent her money like he's supposed to then none of this would have –"

"You're just like him, aren't you?" Dan said. "Your dad, I mean."

Blake's mouth fell open. What the hell was Dan talking about?

"Yeah, you go on about what an arsehole he is, but if you think about it, you're just the same."

"What?"

"Too much of a coward to face up to your mistakes." Dan took another step away from Blake. "You'd rather blame everyone else than deal with the problem."

"And how do I do that?" Blake asked.

"Ignore Vilman and play the Final to win. That's the right thing to do."

Dan turned and walked away.

Blake stared after him until he couldn't see Dan any more. Dan just didn't get it. Mr Vilman would hurt Mum if Blake didn't play to lose. Blake knew it.

He slumped to the ground. It was damp and cold, but Blake didn't care. At first he worried that Dan might tell Coach, or some other grown-up, about the bribe. Then, as the evening went on, Blake kept coming back to what Dan had said about him being like Dad. Dan said he was a coward who blamed everyone else for his mistakes.

Was that true? No. Dan didn't understand.

Blake felt terrible. He stayed sitting under the tree until it was very late and all the distant voices had died away. Only when it started to rain did he get up and walk slowly home.

Chapter 8
The Final

Dan ignored Blake for the next few days. At first Blake worried Dan was going to tell Coach what he'd found out. He knew how important winning the Final was to Dan. But Dan said nothing. Blake found out why on the morning of the Final.

Dan came up to him as the team met in the practice grounds, ready for the drive across town to the new stadium.

"So how's it going?" he said.

Blake shrugged. "Speaking to me now, are you?"

"I thought I'd give you a few days to think about ... about everything," Dan said. "I nearly went to Coach but if I tell on you, you'll be dropped from the team. And we need you. You're the best striker Holton City Colts have had in years. Plus, you want to win the Final. Don't you, Blake? You want to win?"

Blake stared at him. And in that moment he saw that Dan would never understand what he was going through. Dan had his comfortable home and his fancy new video phone. He could afford to see things in black and white. But Blake knew that life wasn't as easy as that. Blake knew that sometimes you had to do things you didn't want to do, to make sure of something else more important.

He had to play the match and he had to make sure his team lost, even though he hated doing it. Protecting Mum was more important.

"Of course I want City Colts to win, Dan, you prat," Blake said. *I just can't let it happen*, he thought to himself.

Dan grinned. "I knew it."

****

As they drew up outside the stadium, Blake felt calmer than he had done for weeks. At least now he knew what he was going to do. As they walked through the gates, Blake saw Mr Vilman standing to one side, watching him.

Blake made sure Dan wasn't looking, then gave Mr Vilman the thumbs up. Mr Vilman nodded.

The stadium was even more impressive in daylight than on the evening Dan and Blake had broken in. They arrived early, so Coach gave them a quick tour. Every part of the building shone with fresh paint. There were the covered stands and VIP areas inside. There was even a booth for the announcer, complete with state-of-the-art sound system. And downstairs the showering and changing areas were amazing. It was all so much smarter than Blake was used to.

"Hey, Blake." Dan rushed up. "We've just heard, there's a proper talent scout out there.

Coach says he's looking out for kids our age to put onto bigger teams."

But before Blake had time to say anything, Coach called him over.

"Bad news, son," Coach said. "I've left it to the last minute to decide, but I'm subbing you for the first half."

"What?" Blake couldn't believe what he was hearing. "Why? Who's taking my place?"

"I'm putting Fred Smith on the right-hand side. He's been playing brilliant all week and, well, you've been off-form since before the Semi."

"But ..."

"No buts, Blake. You know this is going to be a tough game. You're good, sure. But I need everyone right at the top of their form. We'll put you on at half-time."

Blake spent the next hour in a state of shock. He didn't even worry about Mr Vilman. He was just too upset that he wasn't opening the game.

The match began. Blake sat on the side-lines. As he watched Dan and Fred and the others play, he started to think again about having to play badly. The team wanted to win so much. Every part of Blake's body wanted that too.

God, why was this so difficult?

About 20 minutes into the game, the score was still nil-nil. Mr Vilman walked over.

"Why are you on the bench?" he whispered to Blake.

Blake shrugged. "They're giving another striker a chance. But Coach says I'll be on at half-time."

Mr Vilman swore under his breath. "Make sure you are."

Another 20 minutes passed. Coach, who had been watching and yelling from the touch-line, walked over to Blake. "Nip down the changing room, for me, there's a good lad. I left my clip-board down there by the lockers."

Blake raced downstairs. Most of the first half had been pretty boring – neither side was playing to attack – but he still didn't want to miss any of the match. He found the clip-board right away and turned to leave, but tripped over Dan's back pack.

Annoyed, Blake picked the bag up. Dan's new video phone fell out of the front pocket.

Dan was such an idiot sometimes. It was stupid leaving his mobile lying about like that.

Footsteps sounded just outside the changing room.

"But I'll go to jail if this comes out." It was Mr Vilman's voice.

Blake froze.

"Well, this is your last chance to pay me back. You've got till six this evening." It was the man Blake had overheard that first night.

"No problem," Mr Vilman said with relief.

"So, how are you going to get me the money?" the other voice asked.

Mr Vilman muttered something Blake couldn't hear, then said, "OK, I'll explain. Listen to this."

Blake shifted silently from foot to foot. He needed to get out of here without being spotted and make it back up to Coach. He had to be ready to play later.

To play badly.

His heart sank. He so wished there was another way. Dan's mobile was still lying on the floor. Blake bent down to pick it up.

"It's like this ..." Mr Vilman said from the next room.

Blake's fingers curled round the phone.

Of course. There was another way.

And that way was in his hands.

Chapter 9
The Break-in

The whistle blew for half-time. Blake burst onto the pitch. He crashed into Dan.

"Watch my freakin' leg, will you?" Dan said grumpily.

"Come with me." Blake grabbed Dan's arm. "I've worked out what to do."

"Do about what?" Dan pulled away. The other players were streaming past them, heading for the tunnels. "Stop it, man. I can't go anywhere. Neither can you. Coach'll freak out if we're not straight down the changing rooms."

"Oi, Blake." Coach strode over, his face grim. "Where the hell've you been?" He grabbed the clip-board from Blake's hand. "Might as well have fetched this myself. Come on, both of you. Blake, you're straight on after the break."

"Just need a pee," Blake said.

Coach grunted, then turned and walked away. Dan started to follow him but Blake grabbed his arm again.

"I need your help, Dan," he said.

Dan narrowed his eyes. "You've got a nerve, asking me to help you. Don't you think I've helped you enough by pointing out what an idiot you were to take Vilman's money?"

"Yes," Blake said. "You have helped me. And what you told me to do was right. That's why I need your help. I've worked out how to do it all – deal with Vilman and play the Final to win – but there isn't much time. Come on."

"Come on where?" Dan let himself be dragged along a few steps then stopped again.

Blake saw he was going to have to explain his plan. As he did so, Dan stared at him.

"You're mad," Dan said, but he sounded impressed.

Blake stopped. Maybe Dan was right. "D'you think it'll work?" he asked.

Dan's face split into a huge grin. "Only one way to find out."

They raced across the pitch and onto the stand. They flew up the stairs, up to the announcer's booth at the very top of the terrace.

Blake waited to catch his breath. The sound system was blaring out from loud speakers on top of the booth, making half-time announcements about lost children and badly parked cars. There was a small window beside the booth door. The announcer was sitting inside. He had bright red hair and wore a leather jacket.

Blake looked across at Dan. "Here goes." He tried the door handle. Damn. The booth was locked. He banged on the door.

The announcer didn't seem to hear him. At last he finished speaking and looked round. He looked shocked to see Blake hammering on the door, then made a throat-cutting sign with his finger to tell Blake to shut up.

Blake banged harder.

The announcer put down his piece of paper and touched some switches on the panel in front of him. He stood up and walked across.

Blake stopped banging as the door opened. The announcer frowned.

"What the hell ...?"

"It's your car," Blake stammered. "Some bloke sent me up here to tell you there were some kids spraying paint on it outside."

"What?" The announcer's eyes opened wide. "Has anyone called the police?"

Blake glanced at Dan. Dan shrugged.

"Dunno."

The announcer raced off. Blake and Dan nipped inside the booth and shut the door. Suddenly all the background noise from outside stopped.

"Wow, it's sound-proofed," Dan said.

"Lock the door." Blake headed for the sound system in the corner of the room. The booth wasn't big – a couple of metres square with a desk and chair at the far end. The sound system looked really complicated. There was a huge panel of knobs and switches on the desk.

Above the desk was a window overlooking the pitch. Blake clocked what a great view it gave, then sat down at the panel. Man! What were all those switches for?

Dan slid two bolts across the door then raced to join him.

"Go on," he said. "Second half starts in ten minutes and if we're not on the pitch, none of this'll be worth it."

"I know," Blake groaned. "But look at all these knobs and stuff. I don't know which one to use."

Dan leaned over and flicked a large switch. He leaned into the microphone on the table. "Hello? Hello?"

"How do we know if it's working?" Blake said.

"Shouldn't a light come on or something?" Dan asked.

"I don't know." Blake paused. "Look, you go outside and wave through the window if you can hear me."

It felt like a waste of precious seconds to unlock and re-lock the door. At last, Dan was outside and Blake was back at the sound system control panel. He sat down. Just take this step by step, he told himself.

He flicked back the switch Dan had touched.

"Hello?" he said into the microphone.

Outside, Dan shook his head.

Crap. The clock on the panel showed only six minutes until the second half began. Blake began working his way across the knobs and switches on the panel. "Hello?" he kept saying as he pressed each switch. "Hello?"

But Dan kept shaking his head. Clearly no one outside could hear Blake yet. He reached the end of the top line of switches and started on the next one down. Three minutes until the second half.

"Hello?" Blake looked up to see if Dan could hear him this time.

Oh, no. The announcer was back, and he didn't look happy. His face had a deep frown and his mouth was opening and shutting very fast, like he was shouting.

Dan stood next to the announcer, mouthing, "Hurry up."

"I'm trying," Blake muttered. His heart pounded as he flicked the next switch. Nothing. And the next. Still nothing. He glanced over at the window again. The announcer's face was now as red as his hair. Other people had come up beside and behind him. And there was Mr Vilman, pushing his way through the crowd.

Blake felt sick. He turned back to the panel. Come *on*.

A huge thud shook the whole booth. Then another. The door groaned. Oh, God. They were trying to break in.

Blake's heart was in his mouth now. He turned to the panel again. He wished he knew what he was looking for.

There. A switch at the top of the panel he hadn't seen before.

Thump. The booth shook again.

Blake flicked the switch. A light beside the switch shone red.

"Hello?" he shouted into the microphone. Outside he could see people in their seats turning round. The PA system was working.

He glanced over at the window by the door again. There was no sign of Dan. Mr Vilman's face was pressed up against the glass. Another thump against the door.

It was now or never.

Blake's throat was dry as he reached for the microphone.

Chapter 10
The Final Fix

"I'm Blake Johnson. I play for Holton City Colts. In fact ..." Blake looked out of the long window. Both teams were on the pitch, staring up at the announcer's booth. "In fact I should be playing right now. But I'm here because of a man called Martin Vilman who ... who ... well, listen for yourselves. I just taped his conversation in the changing rooms."

Blake reached into his pocket and pulled out Dan's phone. He held the mobile to the microphone and pressed play.

"I told you, I'll give you your money once I've won my bet." Mr Vilman's voice sounded tense and angry.

"And what makes you so sure you'll win your bet?" Another voice. Angry and male. Outside the window, people were staring, open-mouthed up at the booth.

"Because the boy promised me he'll make sure City Colts lose."

"Which boy? How?"

Blake glanced at the door again. It was cracking along one side. Thump. And again. Thump. There wasn't much time.

"His name's Blake Johnson. Holton City Colts' best striker. I've given him money to throw the game. Some already. More after the match is over. It's in the sodding bag," Mr Vilman said.

Crash. With an almighty thump the door caved in. Blake jumped out of his seat. People stormed towards him. But Blake could only see Mr Vilman, his eyes bulging out, his face scarlet.

"You sodding little ... I'll get you for this." He grabbed Blake by his football shirt.

"Not so fast." Coach pushed Vilman away. "Get your hands off my player."

Blake stared as the two men squared up to each other. More people crowded in. Everyone was shouting.

Dan squeezed past. "It worked," he yelled over the noise. "It worked. Everyone heard."

Yes! Blake couldn't believe it. He was in the clear. "We did it!" he shouted.

"Stop. Get him," Coach yelled.

Blake turned. Mr Vilman was pushing past people, heading for the door. And there was Mum, in the doorway. Her eyes were darting everywhere, looking for Blake.

Blake's felt sick. Mum must have heard his broadcast, along with everyone else. What was she going to think? She pushed her way towards him. Coach let her pass.

"Blake." Her whole face was twisted with worry. "Oh, Blake, is ... is that where the money for the rent came from?"

He couldn't look at her. He hung his head and nodded.

"You were going to lose the match for money?" Blake could hear the shock in Coach's voice now. "That's what you were talking to that man – Vilman – about, the other day?"

Blake couldn't bear it. "I'm sorry," he stammered, "but I'm not ... I mean, I didn't go through with it. I ... I couldn't."

Silence.

"Blake?" Mum said. "Look at me."

He looked up.

"What you did was wrong," Mum paused, "but I know you were trying to help me, which ... which means ..." Her voice cracked.

Blake looked over at Coach.

"Well, I think it means you're a bloody idiot." Coach shook his head. "But we can discuss all that later. You'd better get on that pitch now. And make sure you play to win this time."

"Yes, Coach." Blake raced down onto the pitch with Dan. For a few minutes everyone crowded round, talking about what had happened. The other players looked at Blake like they couldn't believe he'd nearly taken the bribe.

Blake looked out into the stands. Where had Mr Vilman gone? He must have got out of the booth while Mum and Coach were talking. Blake felt uneasy.

Then Coach strode over and took him to one side.

"Just wanted to let you know, son," he said. "I've rung the police. They're on their way to arrest Vilman now. They'll want to talk to you too, but put all that out of your mind for now." He pointed to the pitch. "We've got a game to win."

For the first few minutes of the second half, Blake didn't think he was going to be able to focus. His head was buzzing from everything that had happened. And then he got his first touch of the ball and felt free, like he always did when he played. He raced up and down the pitch like a bullet, creating chances and taking shots whenever he could. He scored twice – a nice header off a perfectly weighted pass from Dan. And then the winning goal – a scissor-kick volley which sailed between two defenders, smack into the net.

The crowd roared. Blake was covered with hugs from his team mates. And then Dan came up.

"Nice one," he grinned, as everyone else jogged back towards their starting positions. "I knew you wouldn't let us down."

Blake shrugged. He felt embarrassed. "Thanks," he said. "Yeah. And, nice pass … er, thanks, man. For everything."

"No sweat."

The game finished with City Colts winning by two goals to one. They'd won the Final!

****

The next few hours passed in a blur. Blake's team mates and Coach told him he was a prat for taking Mr Vilman's money, but that they forgave him because he'd won the trophy for them. Then Blake had to speak to the local police and tell them exactly what Mr Vilman had asked him to do. A few hours after that, news came that Mr Vilman had been arrested.

The next day, Coach dropped by to tell Blake and Mum that Mr Vilman had a long string of other offences against his name.

"Which means he's going down this time. Blake's still got to talk to the cops again, but everyone's safe," Coach said, looking at Mum. He cleared his throat. "Now, d'you want the good news?"

Blake looked up. "There's more?"

Coach smiled. "Remember the talent scout who was in the crowd yesterday? Well, he wants you to play for United's under-18 team. It's a big challenge, but there's money in it so you'll be earning from the start. It's a great chance to work your way up to the big league."

Blake sat there. He didn't know what to think or say. United Juniors. A Championship League Junior team. It was more than fantastic. It was the best thing that had ever happened to him.

He turned to Mum. "I'll be able to help with the rent properly now," he said.

Mum looked like she might be about to cry, so Blake hurried on. There'd been something on his mind ever since he'd told everyone the truth about the match fixing.

"What about the £300 Vilman gave me?" he said to Coach. "Do I have to pay that back?"

"Don't worry about that, son." Coach looked at Mum. "The lawyers are arguing over it but I've covered the money for now – you can pay me back when you can."

"Oh." Mum's voice cracked. Her eyes filled up. "I don't know how we can ever thank you," she said at last.

Coach looked alarmed. "Er ... no need to thank me," he said gruffly. "Seeing Blake play his best will be all the thanks I need." He turned to go. "But don't forget, Blake, there's still a black mark against your name. You're going to have to be squeaky clean from now on. The Club bosses have their eye on you. Think you can handle that?"

Blake nodded, a huge grin on his face. After Coach had gone, he went upstairs to call Dan.

Five minutes later he was shooting out the door. He headed for the park, only one thing on his mind.

Football.

Football forever.

Our books are tested
for children and young people by
children and young people.

Thanks to everyone who consulted on
a manuscript for their time and effort in
helping us to make our books better
for our readers.